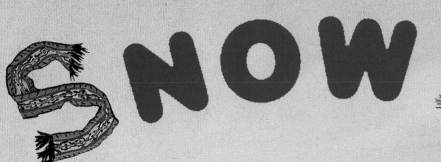

SNOW DAY

MOIRA FAIN

WALKER AND COMPANY
NEW YORK

First published in the United States of America in 1996
by Walker Publishing Company, Inc; first paperback edition published in 1998.

Published simultaneously in Canada by Thomas Allen & Son Canada, Limited, Markham, Ontario

Library of Congress Cataloging-in-Publication Data
Fain, Moira.
Snow day/Moira Fain.
p. cm.
Summary: Although Sister Agatha Ann asks her to write a poem, Maggie wants to draw it instead;
a day of playing together in the snow resolves the dilemma.
ISBN 0-8027-8409-7 (hardcover). —ISBN 0-8027-8410-0 (reinforced)
[1. Drawing—Fiction. 2. Snow—Fiction. 3. Schools—Fiction.]
I. Title.
PZ7.F145Sn   1996
[E]—dc20   95-49586
CIP
AC

ISBN 0-8027-7551-9 (paperback)

Book design by Eleen Cheung

Printed in Hong Kong
10 9 8 7 6 5 4 3 2 1

For my children

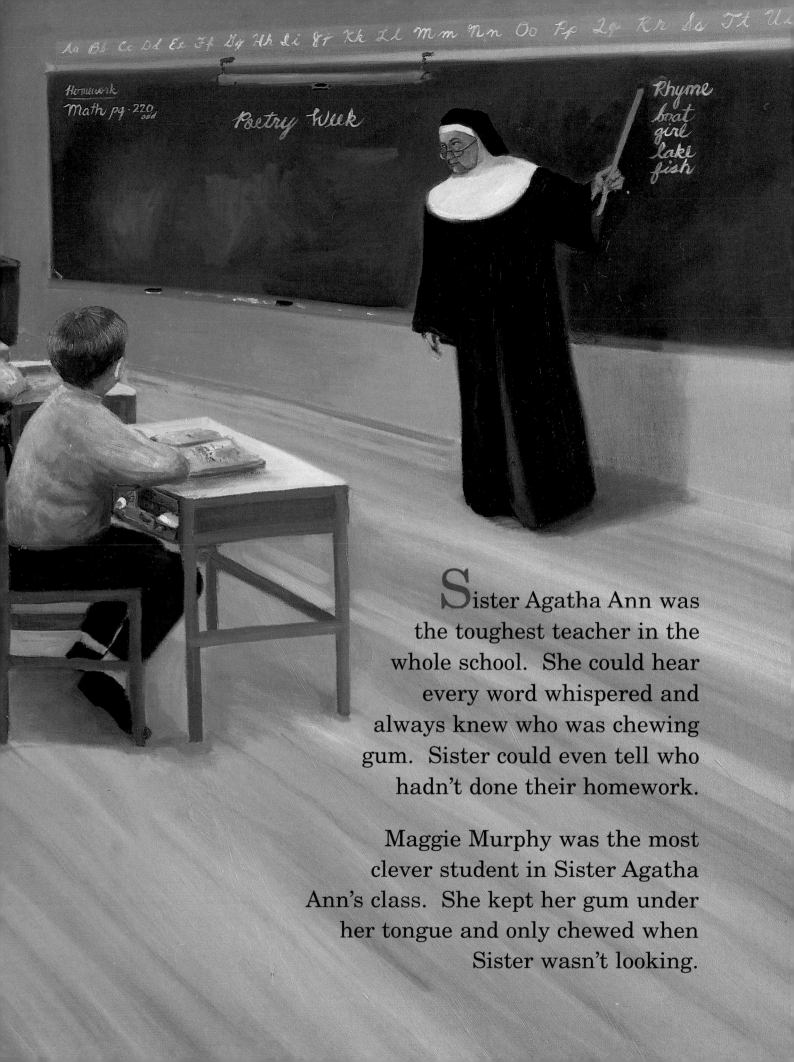

Sister Agatha Ann was the toughest teacher in the whole school. She could hear every word whispered and always knew who was chewing gum. Sister could even tell who hadn't done their homework.

Maggie Murphy was the most clever student in Sister Agatha Ann's class. She kept her gum under her tongue and only chewed when Sister wasn't looking.

Sister Agatha Ann never caught Maggie whispering because Maggie sent notes instead. And with each secret note she would draw a picture. Maggie could draw horses and trees; she could even draw people.

One day when the rest of the class was busy writing poems, Maggie began to draw and forgot to watch for Sister Agatha Ann.

"Young lady, you have made a terrible mistake," announced Sister Agatha Ann. "WE do not deface school property in THIS classroom." Maggie's pen had slipped off the page, smearing ink onto her desk.

"Go get a bucket of soapy water and clean this mess." The rest of the class began to laugh and Maggie could feel her cheeks turn red. "You will have to write your poem for homework and recite it for the class tomorrow," said Sister in a voice that made the room fall silent.

After supper Maggie went to her bedroom to do her homework. She sat at her desk and stared out the window. It was almost Christmas and the ground was still bare. "I can write a poem about snow," she thought. "That will be easy."

But giggles echoed in the hallway and suddenly her brother Matthew appeared at her door. "We have a surprise for you," he teased.

"PILLOW FIGHT!" Maggie ran for her pillow and pummeled her brothers and sisters until Mom and Dad came to put them to bed.

That night Maggie tossed and turned, worrying about her unfinished homework. A winter chill swept through the bedroom and she pulled her blanket over her head. "I'm never coming out, not ever," she decided before falling asleep.

The weatherman's voice on her clock radio woke Maggie the next morning. "Go back to bed, folks. Last night's snowstorm was a humdinger. Our list of school closings begins with Saint Bridget's . . ."

"SNOW DAY!"

Maggie threw off her blanket and ran to the window.
Her neighborhood was covered in deep, blue softness, as if
every cloud in the sky had fallen to the ground.

Everyone raced through breakfast
while Mom pulled snowsuits from a
box in the closet. Christopher wore a
heavy sweater because his old snowsuit
fit Maggie now. Her snowsuit fit Lisa,
Lisa's snowsuit fit Regina, and Regina's
fit Matt. Last year's outfit still fit
Jonathan just fine.

A truck the color of a Christmas tree pushed a mountain of snow all the way to the end of the driveway. They had just started to dig a tunnel when Freddie Doulin interrupted.

"Hey, Maggie," he called. "We're all going sledding on School Hill. How 'bout it?"

"I'm not going to school today," Maggie yelled back. "I didn't do my homework."

"It's a SNOW DAY." Freddie laughed. "No school means no teachers. Come on!"

School Hill had changed to a
mountain of sparkling powder
that promised the best sled ride
ever. "I guess I'll go first."
Freddie gulped. He picked up his
sled and walked to the edge.

"STOP WHERE YOU ARE!" boomed a familiar voice. It was Sister Agatha Ann! "Sister Katherine and Sister Anastasia were just saying how much fun it would be to have a sled race."

Maggie pulled down the rim of her hat, hoping that Sister Agatha Ann wouldn't recognize her. "Maggie Murphy," said Sister, "your sled is just my size."

She took the rope from Maggie's hands and they all trudged through the snow to the very peak of the hill.

After they settled onto the sled, Sister called out, "On your mark, get set, GO!" Icy snow stung Maggie's cheeks as she and Sister careened down the hill. "Look out for the bump!" called Sister Agatha Ann as they flew into the air and slammed back down onto the snow. But they stayed on the sled all the way to the bottom.

Maggie leaped off and looked around for the others. "WE WON!" she cried.

Maggie's teacher rose from the sled covered with snow and Maggie giggled at the sight.

"How did the homework go last night?" asked Sister. "Do you have a poem to share with the class?"

"No," squeaked Maggie. "I drew a picture instead."

Sister Agatha Ann frowned for a moment or two and then spouted, "I would like to draw a picture for you, Maggie, but I'm going to draw my picture with words.

"When I was young, the snow was deeper
And all the hills seemed so much steeper.
The crusty ice I walked upon
Would never once give in,
And every sled race that I ran
Would surely be a win.
It's good to see the snow again
From a child's point of view,
Because what you see is different
When you're a bigger you."

The next morning when Sister Agatha Ann called on Maggie to read her poem, she handed her a box of colored chalk. "You may draw a picture on the blackboard to illustrate your poem."

As Maggie pulled her piece of chalk across the board she sang out:

> "Snow is like the blanket
> That lies upon my bed,
> Mountain peaks like sugar hills
> Are really my knees instead.
>
> I dreamed that spring had come
> And snow would fall no more.
> 'Wake up, you sleepyhead,
> Your blanket's on the floor.'"

Sister Agatha Ann left Maggie's drawing on the blackboard for the rest of the day.